Moving Day!

Robert Munsch

Illustrations by
Michael Martchenko

North Winds Press
An Imprint of Scholastic Canada Ltd.

The art for this book was painted in watercolour on Crescent illustration board.
The type is set in 19 point Charter Roman.

Library and Archives Canada Cataloguing in Publication

Munsch, Robert N., 1945-, author
Moving day! / by Robert Munsch ; illustrated by Michael Martchenko.

ISBN 978-1-4431-6398-9 (hardcover)

I. Martchenko, Michael, illustrator II. Title.

PS8576.U575M68 2018   jC813'.54   C2018-902137-3

www.scholastic.ca

6 5 4 3 2 1   Printed in Canada 119   18 19 20 21 22

MIX
Paper from
responsible sources
FSC® C103113
FSC
www.fsc.org

To Danielle Vroom,
Montreal, Quebec.
— R.M.

For Mindy, the best little dog ever.
— M.M.

On moving day, Danielle's mother and father were running around and putting everything into boxes.

Her dad was yelling, "The moving truck is coming, the moving truck is coming!"

Her mom was yelling, "In boxes, in boxes! Everything in boxes!"

Danielle was standing in the middle of the living room, wondering what to do.

Her mother said, "Danielle, don't just stand there. Do something. Pack something. Take care of the little kids. Take care of your little sister."

"Okay," said Danielle.

Julianne was playing in her bedroom. Danielle picked her up, put her in a box with some pillows, and taped it all around.

Her mother came by and said, "Danielle, did you take care of your little sister?"

"Definitely taken care of," said Danielle.

"Good. Well, do something else. Take care of your little brother."

"Right," said Danielle.

She went and found her brother
and said, "How are you doing,
Christopher?"

"I'm doing fine," said Christopher.

"Good," said Danielle. She picked
him up and put him in another box
with some blankets. She packed towels
all around and taped it up.

Her mother came by and said, "Oh, Danielle, you are being so quiet and so nice. Have you taken care of Julianne and Christopher?"

"Oh yes," said Danielle, "I've taken care of them just fine."

"Good," said her mother. "Well, pack something else up. Go help Laurin."

So Danielle went up to Laurin's room. She pushed Laurin into a box of stuffed animals, covered her up with the toys, and taped it all over.

Then Danielle went to her mom and said, "I'm done with Laurin. What should I do now?"

"Go help Rylan," said her mom.

15

Danielle went into Rylan's room. Rylan was standing in the middle, singing.

"Now that's useful," said Danielle, and she pushed Rylan into a box of sweaters. Rylan said all kinds of horrible things and Danielle didn't say anything.

17

Finally the truck came and the movers were taking out the boxes. Danielle's mother said, "Danielle, you are being so quiet and all the other kids are being so quiet. You did a wonderful job with them. Where are they?"

"In the boxes," said Danielle. "I packed them in boxes and taped them all up."

"OH NO!" said her mother. "We have to stop and get them out!"

19

But her dad said, "Wait a minute. The moving truck is here and we can't stop. We'll get them out at the other end."

So they jumped into the car and followed the truck down the road to the new house.

They got all the boxes out and piled them up.

Danielle's mom and dad looked at the boxes and said, "So, where are they?"

"Well," said Danielle, "you've just got to listen."

She put her ear to one box and heard "La-la, la-la, la-la," and she said, "That's Julianne. She's in there. She's singing."

Her mom opened the box, and Julianne was fine.

Danielle listened to another box and heard "Thumpy-thump, thumpy-thump, thumpy-thump." She said, "Ohhh, that must be Christopher, he's kicking."

Her dad opened the box, and Christopher was fine.

Danielle listened to another box and heard "Zzzz, zzzz, zzzz, zzzz." She said, "That's Laurin, she's sleeping."

Her mother opened the box, and Laurin was fine.

Danielle listened to another box and heard someone yelling, "I'M GOING TO GET YOU! YOU'RE GOING TO PAY!" and she said, "That's Rylan. He's mad about something."

Her father opened the box, and Rylan was fine.

And her parents had lots of time to unpack because the little kids spent the next three days chasing Danielle, trying to put HER into a box.

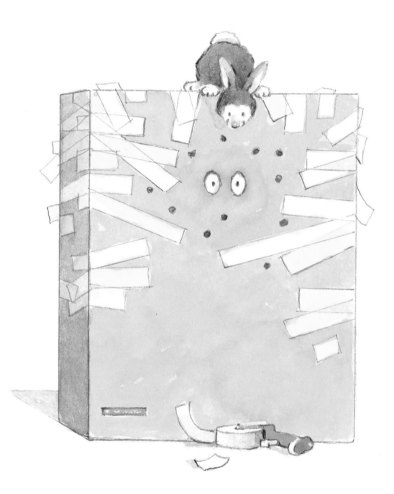